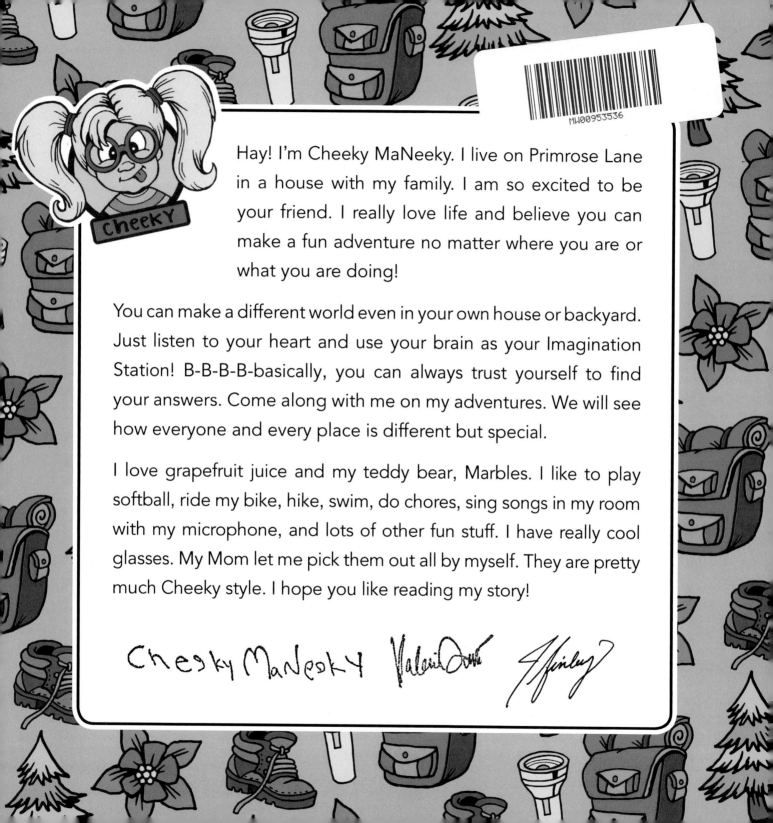

Hay! I'm Cheeky MaNeeky. I live on Primrose Lane in a house with my family. I am so excited to be your friend. I really love life and believe you can make a fun adventure no matter where you are or what you are doing!

You can make a different world even in your own house or backyard. Just listen to your heart and use your brain as your Imagination Station! B-B-B-B-basically, you can always trust yourself to find your answers. Come along with me on my adventures. We will see how everyone and every place is different but special.

I love grapefruit juice and my teddy bear, Marbles. I like to play softball, ride my bike, hike, swim, do chores, sing songs in my room with my microphone, and lots of other fun stuff. I have really cool glasses. My Mom let me pick them out all by myself. They are pretty much Cheeky style. I hope you like reading my story!

Cheeky MaNeeky®
GOES TO COLORADO

CREATED BY
The Spirit and Imagination of Valerie D'Ann Doshier

Written by D'Ann Swain

Illustrated by Artistic Genius Joshua Finley

Graphic Design by Amanda Wilde

On a sunny summer day, Finn and I are in the backyard helping Cheeky and Finn's mom plant a small tree.

Mom says, "Finn, where is your sister? She wanted to help us plant this tree."

"I bet she is doing Cheeky stuff," replies Finn. "I'll go find her!"

About this time, Cheeky bounds out the backdoor completely dressed in hiking clothes—Cheeky-style!

"Cheeky, why are you dressed like that?" says Finn, laughing at all her gear.

Cheeky says, "This little tree makes me think of a hike we went on one time to… to… hummm… I think it was called… Max's water-is-falling or… or sumtheeen like that!"

Finn, Mom, and I look at each other puzzled.

Then, Mom says, "Cheeky, do you mean Maxwell Falls in Colorado?"

"Narf, narf! Chure, that's it!"

Finn fills the hole with water to get ready for the new tree.

"I really want to hike there and talk to the animals," Cheeky says. "Pencil Toes, will you take us there for an adventure? PLEEEEZ?!"

We all agree that it would be a fun adventure for today, so I use my magic pencil toes and draw the magic door. Cheeky, Finn, and I step through the door as Cheeky squeals with excitement.

"HUP HUP HUPPEEEN! Let's go!" Cheeky exclaims.

We step through the magic door and onto the hiking trail to begin our hike.

"Maybe we can pet some of the animals! Let's look for some," decides Cheeky.

As we are walking along, Cheeky looks up the trail and sees someone.

"Look, guys!" she says. "There is a lady sitting in the forest painting a picture. Let's go talk to her."

Finn and I agree to go see what the lady is doing. As we get closer, we see her sitting there with her paint and a big canvas.

"Cheeky says to the lady, "Hi there! My name is Cheeky MaNeeky. This is my brother, Finn, and my dog, Pencil Toes! Whatchya doin'?"

The lady looks up from her easel and paints and says, "Well, hello there. My name is Valerina. It is nice to meet you. I come to the forest often to paint pictures."

As the three of us are looking at her painting, three birds fly up and perch on the top of the painting.

Valerina greets them, "Well, good morning my little bird family!"

Cheeky looks at the birds in amazement and says, "These birds are your family?"

"Oh yes," Valerina replies. "They keep me company while I paint. They are my forest family. Let me introduce you to them. This is Tennessee. She is an orange-breasted robin. She loves to sing."

Tennessee belts out a lovely tune for us!

Cheeky takes her flashlight out of her belt, acting like it is a microphone, and says, "Me too, me too! I like to sing in my room with my microphone!"

Valerina smiles at Cheeky and her flashlight-turned-microphone. "This is Louisa. She is a blue jay. She has a really big smile and is very busy and energetic."

Finn says, smiling, "She is just like you, Cheeky—full of life and energy!"

Louisa blurts out with a big smile, "Yep, that's me. I keep things exciting around here!"

Valerina says, "My other friend is Scarlet. She is a lark. She is very proper, and she is the state bird of Colorado."

Cheeky exclaims, "Wow, the state bird? That sounds important."

Scarlet takes her wing, adjusts her necklace, and says, "It is very nice to meet all of you."

Louisa chimes in and says, "Yep, we call her Scar Scar!"

Valerina asks, "Cheeky, what are you guys doing here at Maxwell Falls today?"

"Well, we came on an adventure all the way from Primrose Lane. I want to hike to the water-is-falling, and I want to pet some of the animals in the forest!"

Finn says, "Now Cheeky, I am not so sure we should get close to any of the animals."

"Yes, that is correct, Finn," adds Valerina. "We must stay a safe distance from them. This is their home, and we must be very respectful to them. Some of them are very big like the elk I am painting. They have very big antlers and stand tall and strong."

Cheeky looks at the painting as she pushes up her pink glasses and asks, "Is the elk hiding behind the tree?"

Valerina goes on to explain, "Well yes, Cheeky… in a way. If we don't respect the animals and their home then the animals will slowly disappear, and that would be sad."

Then, Scarlet the lark says to us, "Always remember to keep a safe distance from any animals out here."

Louisa says, with that big blue jay smile, "Yep, yep! That's right, Scar Scar, you got it! Hey Tennessee, you should make up a song about that!"

Tennessee begins to sing in her very best robin voice:

Be safe, be safe
and
Keep our home clean, keep our home clean!

Finn says, "Yeah! You know, Cheeky, we have our reusable water bottles so we don't have all that plastic trash. That is being responsible and taking care of the Earth."

"Yes, Finn, you are correct again," agrees Valerina. "When we do the right things for each other and the planet, we feel good about ourselves."

"Mom and Dad say we should leave the planet better than we found it!" chimes in Cheeky.

"That's right, Cheeky," says Finn. "Just like today when we planted the small tree in the backyard."

"Cheeky, I see you have a teddy bear in your backpack," says Valerina.

"Oh yeah, this is my bear, Marbles. She goes everywhere with me! She loves to hike."

Valerina continues, "Well, she is very special, but remember—you wouldn't want to get close to a real bear in the forest, so be careful on your hike to the waterfalls."

So Cheeky, Finn, and I head up the trail toward the waterfalls. As we walk along, we talk about being careful and watching out for animals along the way.

Finn says, "I love the forest. It is so quiet and pretty. Look at all the trees and flowers."

"Yeah," agrees Cheeky. "It is the best place to dream in magic."

As we approach the waterfalls, we stop to listen to the sound of the falling water. About that time, Cheeky spots a deer getting a drink from the waterfall pool.

She shrieks loudly, "Oh my goose, look! There is a deer!"

"Shhhh, Cheeky," Finn whispers. "We don't want to scare the deer!"

"I wish I could pet that deer!"

I grab ahold of Cheeky's untied tennis shoestring to keep her still because we all know how excited Cheeky can get.

"Well, you can get your camera out of your pocket and take a picture of her," Finn says. "I bet she won't mind that!"

Cheeky grabs her camera and snaps a few pictures. The three of us stand there quietly and watch the deer and the other animals that begin to gather at the pool.

"Look, Finn! Here come Tennessee, Scarlet, and Louisa!" Cheeky exclaims. "What are you little birdies doing here?"

Scarlet replies, "We thought we would come to the pool for a drink of water and check up on you guys."

Louisa chirps with her big smile, "Yep, yep! We look out for each other here in the forest. That's what families do."

Tennessee chimes in, "Yes, and sometimes I belt out a song to warn our friends if we think there is danger."

Cheeky says, "Finn, they are like us—we always look out for each other!"

"This pool sure is clean," Louisa says as she guzzles some water.

Scarlet replies, "Yes, it is so important to keep the forest clean for us. It is our home!"

"Cheeky, do you know what that means to us?" asks Finn.

I pick up an old plastic water bottle I find on the trail and bring it to Cheeky.

Cheeky exclaims, "Chure! Of course! We need to take our trash with us when we head for home!"

It is starting to get late in the afternoon, so we decide to head back down the trail hoping to see our new friend Valerina. As we arrive back at the spot where Valerina is painting, we see she is still there, and her bird family is there with her.

Cheeky says, "Well, Valerina, we think we better head back home. Mom might need our help with sumtheeen. We sure are glad we met you and your bird family! We love making new friends!"

Finn adds, "Yes, we have a new tree to check on!"

I draw the magic doorway, and we step back through it. Valerina and her bird family wave goodbye.

Scarlet says, "Come back anytime!"

With a big smile, Louisa belts out, "Or maybe we can come see you at Primrose Lane!"

As we step through the magic door and into our backyard, Mom is still tending to the small tree.

Cheeky shrieks, "Mom! Mom! We had a great adventure on our hike. I gotta tell you about our new friends we met in the forest! There was a girl painting a picture and… and her bird family. We cleaned up the forest, saw a deer, and… and…"

Mom looks up from the tree she is tending and says, "Cheeky, I feel like I was on the hike with you. I had three little birds here with me sitting in the new tree while you were gone!"

"Wow, Mom! That's like dreaming in magic. I gotta go tell Dad about this!"

THANKS FOR READING

Hay Friends, Cheeky here!
I hope you enjoyed our trip to Colorado!
Please come along on our next adventure:
"Cheeky MaNeeky Goes To New Mexico"
So until then... Live your life with your
own style! Oh yeah ♡ I hope you will get
my first book, Cheeky MaNeeky Goes To Texas
and one of my coloring books, so you can
color your own world!

HERE'S A LITTLE BIT ABOUT MY FRIENDS AND FAMILY

PENCIL TOES

Pencil Toes is one of my best friends! He is smart and patient with me. He helps keep me on track when my Imagination Station gets a little carried away. He loves adventures and taking care of the Earth. He can take us anywhere we want to go with his magic pencil toes.

MARBLES

Marbles is my teddy bear that my Mom gave me. It was her teddy bear when she was a little girl. Marbles is a good listener and loves to cuddle. She likes to go everywhere with me. She doesn't even mind riding in my backpack!

MOM

My Mom loves me and helps me with lots of stuff. She has taught Finn and me a lot of important things, but mostly she just says, "I love you more than anything." She says that to us everyday!

FINN

Finn is my brother. He is jeeest a little older than me. He is super fun, and he is my bestest friend ever. He likes to wear hats. Finn is very smart and helps me not to get things too complicated. Finn knows a lot about people and things that are good for our health. Finn has a great imagination, too. One smart thing he always says to me is, "Cheeky, sometimes just keeping things easy and simple is a healthy way to spend your day!"

DAD

My Dad loves Finn and me. He helps us take care of our animals. Pencil Toes always gets a hug from Dad. He also teaches us about our chores and responsible stuff.

WORD SEARCH

```
L E H J O S P W B D C Z H P F
V E E Y R L C K D Q Y W C E F
K K Y N I D E A F E B I E N K
L E R Y V A N I R E L A V C T
N E B F S I E A I L T W X I G
R F P O Y N R G C S E Z S L G
R V V R L B C O L Z T T Q T N
C H E E K Y M A N E E K Y O I
Y Y G S U L M D N M A O M E T
I P L T O I I N V O E N I S N
B Z V U N P E V F X P N L U I
D E I A H S F N L M L J T L A
D S Y R S I J W I L Z L V J P
A B V E N N I F E F E W A D O
M Y E F R I E N D S G R Z H T
```

Animals   Cheeky Maneeky   Environment
Finn   Forest   Friends
Lovisa   Painting   Pencil Toes
Scarlet   Tennessee   Valerina

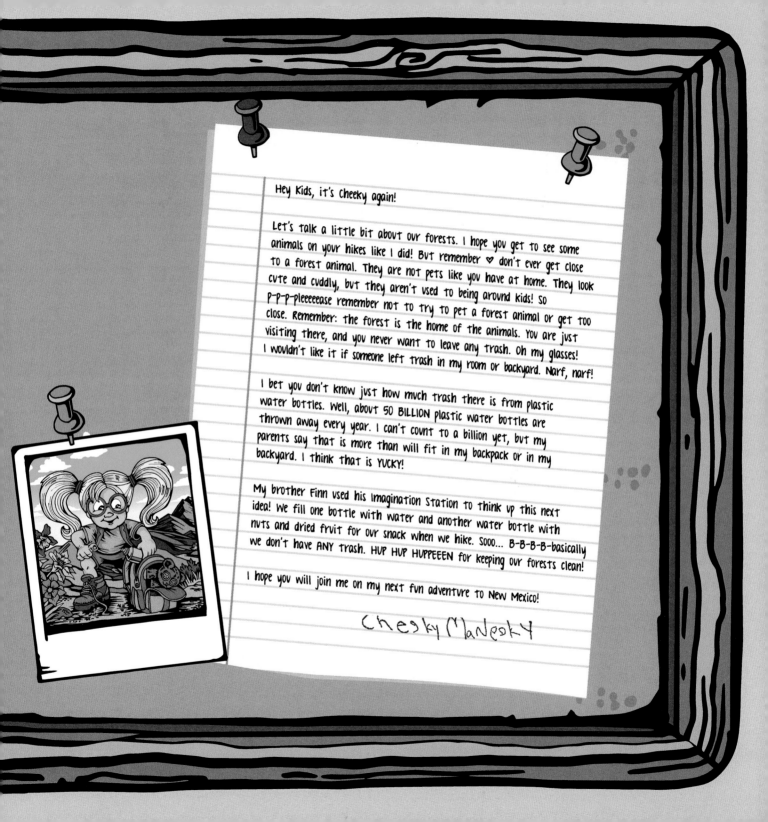

Hey Kids, it's Cheeky again!

Let's talk a little bit about our forests. I hope you get to see some animals on your hikes like I did! But remember ♥ don't ever get close to a forest animal. They are not pets like you have at home. They look cute and cuddly, but they aren't used to being around kids! So p-p-p-pleeeeease remember not to try to pet a forest animal or get too close. Remember: the forest is the home of the animals. You are just visiting there, and you never want to leave any trash. Oh my glasses! I wouldn't like it if someone left trash in my room or backyard. Narf, narf!

I bet you don't know just how much trash there is from plastic water bottles. Well, about 50 BILLION plastic water bottles are thrown away every year. I can't count to a billion yet, but my parents say that is more than will fit in my backpack or in my backyard. I think that is YUCKY!

My brother Finn used his Imagination Station to think up this next idea! We fill one bottle with water and another water bottle with nuts and dried fruit for our snack when we hike. Sooo... B-B-B-B-basically we don't have ANY trash. HUP HUP HUPPEEEN for keeping our forests clean!

I hope you will join me on my next fun adventure to New Mexico!

Cheeky ManesкY

Share your adventures with us!
#CheekyMaNeeky

Find out more at CheekyMaNeeky.com

f 📷

Follow us on Facebook & Instagram!
@cheekymaneeky

Made in the USA
Lexington, KY
10 November 2019

56670156R00033